FINISHING LINE PRESS

www.finishinglinepress.com

CABBIE

New York City 1971,1972

True tales by

N.G. Haiduck

Finishing Line Press
Georgetown, Kentucky

CABBIE

New York City 1971,1972

Publisher: Leah Huete de Maines
Editor: Christen Kincaid
Cover Art: Cole Thornton, Instagram: @swimsinink
Author Photo: Neal Haiduck
Cover Design: Cole Thornton, Instagram: @swimsinink

Order online: www.finishinglinepress.com
also available on amazon.com

Author inquiries and mail orders:
Finishing Line Press
PO Box 1626
Georgetown, Kentucky 40324
USA

Contents

Night Shift 1

Park Avenue 3

Pulling In 5

Halloween 7

Temptation 8

Cabbie 10

Cabbies Dream Too... 12

Eviction 14

La Fille Mal Gardée... 15

Winter 17

Day Shift 20

Stops Along the Way... 22

More Temptation.. 25

Bad Days... 28

Growing Up... 30

"42 Percenter" 32

Plans 33

Just Wait... 35

Author's Notes.. 37

*Dedicated to all those
who have tried to make a living
driving a yellow taxi cab
in New York City*

and

to Annie Garde

To My Readers,

I was a young woman, 20-something, a small town girl new to New York City, living in a two-room apartment on the Lower East Side (the rent was $100 a month) and attending Brooklyn College, which was tuition free in those days. A classmate always had money in his pocket because he was driving a yellow taxi cab. A lot of college guys were driving cabs in those days, but very few women. He persuaded me to try it. This was in 1971.

At the same time, my best friend from Brooklyn College, Annie Garde, had moved to Missoula, Montana (she wanted to leave her childhood home, as I had done). During my cab driving days, I wrote her long letters on my IBM selectric typewriter. Turns out she saved my letters! Many years later, she visited me in New York and presented me with the letters. By then I was teaching at The City College of New York, having earned an M.Ed. from Baruch College and an M.F.A. in poetry from City.

After retirement, I pulled out those letters and confronted my young self—and New York City in the early 1970s. "Cabbie" tells the story of those days. I only used the letters—I could not possibly replicate my youthful voice—and added *Author's Notes* when I thought it necessary for clarification. It is almost a "coming of age" story as I became more savvy, about making money driving a cab, about dealing with difficult customers and my boss (the dispatcher) and unwanted, but sometimes tempting, male suitors, and about planning for a future.

I am delighted that Christen Kincaid, Director and Senior Editor, and Leah Maines, Publisher, of *Finishing Line Press,* have allowed me to share my stories with you. I hope you enjoy reading these chapters of days gone by in New York City from the perspective of a small town girl in a yellow taxi cab.

Sincerely,
N.G. Haiduck

NIGHT SHIFT

Yesterday I got my first paycheck, and I bought a pair of hiking shoes. I had been wearing canvas old ladies shoes, no good in winter. My new shoes are a mustard color and have thick rubber ripple soles and cord shoestrings. They are sturdy and well made. They come up to a bit above my ankle. They are called Tyroleans. Everyone in the taxi garage noticed.

"Oh, so those are the shoes you bought with your first paycheck." I looked pretty funny standing on one leg while everyone took a look at my shoe. They wanted particularly to check out the rubber ripple sole. I am very pleased with myself. Next on the list is a radio.

I'm a big hit at the garage. It's not just that I'm a woman, but that I'm so little. I look like a midget next to these men. Sometimes I need their help, for example, when the car seat doesn't pull up. "Hey, Izzy, give the girl another car; her feet don't reach the pedals and the seat won't pull up." I get another car. "All right, how's that? Your feet reach the pedals?"

I start the night shift at 4:00 in the afternoon. The worst part about this job is the hours. Drivers have to have the car out for nine hours, which means, if I start at 4:00, I can't come back to the garage until 1:00 a.m., although I have been coming in at around 12:30, and Sunday, I really slacked off and brought the car in at 11:30. Sammy didn't say anything, but I can't do this too often because he fired a guy for bringing the cab in too early. Sometimes I don't go into until 5:00 p.m., but then I have to work till 2:00 a.m., but I take breaks in between. And I can take days off anytime I want, except Saturday and Sunday. Everybody has to work Saturday and Sunday.

Between 4:00 and 6:30, I usually drive around Central Park or Gramercy or Washington Square and I am not able to keep my mind on driving, looking at all the people in the park, sweaters and jackets on, the wind blowing in the car, blowing people's hair, blowing the leaves everywhere, out into the streets, under the car tires. People playing instruments in the park, the hotdog vendors, the kids and businessmen and secretaries taking walks in the brisk weather, a policeman on Sixth Avenue always smiling. Every time I see him he's smiling and patting kids on the head. The sun shining. I always notice the sun shining because at that time of day it gets in my eyes when I'm driving. Certain times I can hardly contain myself, and I say to my passengers, "It is a beautiful day!" The passengers feel it too.

My cabbie friend, Jake, said he saw me on Lexington Avenue and his passenger thought I was a gypsy. He said, "Hey, there's a gypsy driving that cab!" I had a scarf around my hair like I always wear and my dangling earrings. Jake said, "Naw, that's just the girl from my garage." All the men at the garage call me "the girl." For example, I need to get into the washroom to pee. "Hey Sammie, the girl wants to get in."

Every time I'm parked at a red light and I look to my right, someone is smiling at me in the next car. I look to my left and the other driver is staring at me in disbelief. I look in front of me and the people crossing the street are staring at me or smiling. Sometimes, a lot of times, people honk their horns and wave to me and smile.

A lot of times people roll down their windows to talk to me. When a man is in another cab, he says, "How come I didn't get you?" Everyone always says, "This is the first time I ever had a woman cabdriver." Sometimes they don't notice at first and when they do, they are startled and say: "Oh my god! It's a girl! A young girl!" They say: "Are you old enough to drive?" "Aren't you afraid?" One old guy said, "For God's sake, don't drive like a girl!" My tips are fantastic.

PARK AVENUE

At night there is no sunshine, of course, and it's colder. Now the people are wearing coats and even boots. I might see a couple, say, on the corner of Park Avenue and 61st Street. The offices are all closed, windows lit up, but the building is still dark, empty, Park Avenue practically deserted. One couple stands on the dark corner dwarfed by the gigantic, magnificent architecture of Park Avenue. The lady has on a long fur coat and she is holding it together because the wind is whipping it around her legs. A scarf is flapping and perfectly set hair is flying out of place, in spite of hair spray. The man, in a tuxedo, holds her with one arm and hails my cab with the other. They are so glad to get inside my cab.

I say, "Didn't it get cold all of a sudden?" They agree. It's real cozy in the back of my cab.

I can't get over the rich ladies who get into my cab—women, my own age too. I pick them up at Park Avenue, Fifth Avenue or Central Park West. They go to places like The Pierre, The Plaza, The New York Athletic Club, Essex House, The Moritz, Delmonicos or some place in the vicinity of Central Park South. Some people have so much money. I don't mean a comfortable income like my grandparents. I mean money, fucking money. And it's not just a few people, a lot of people in New York City have a lot of money. When I first started driving, I thought The Plaza was the Ritz. The Plaza is nothing. But what the hell do I even know about it?

Jake told me about a woman he picked up at Sutton Place who hired him to drive slowly down Fifth Avenue while she window shopped. After window shopping, he drove her to the heliport. The meter read $8 and she gave him a $2 tip.

I can hardly believe someone would throw away $10 like that. Why did she need him to follow her down Fifth? It's not hard to get a cab on Fifth. People spend tons of money just on clothes and cosmetics and hair dressers, let alone taxi cabs, and the expensive hotels where they go to eat dinner.

As soon as a rich woman gets into the cab, I notice the smell. They all wear expensive perfume that smells. And there really are people who put on long gowns and tuxedos, regularly. What really cracks me up is that they are women my age.

One old guy got in the cab at Park Avenue with a young woman, my age. The man had on a tux, the woman wore a long coat. He was distinguished looking and nice too. He took her to a luxury apartment building right off Park Avenue, uptown a little bit. He called her, "the young lady." They got out, he kissed her goodnight, she went inside, and he came back. I drove him back downtown on Park Avenue where I had picked them up. He said, proudly, "That's my daughter."

Then he said, "My son drives a cab." He's been driving a cab for four years, putting himself through college, paying his own tuition. The father was quite proud of him, and I even thought to myself that his son must be all right, to work and go to school when he doesn't have to, and to drive a cab, which is really not the best job in the world.

Actually, some of my favorite passengers are rich older couples. They are so elegant, so confident, so sure of themselves, and usually talkative and friendly and curious about a young girl driving. They give me big tips. They talk to me even after they get out of the cab, telling me to be careful, don't drive too late. They say they think it's wonderful that I have initiative and that I am brave. One old guy called me "a sharp cookie."

When there is a couple in the cab, the woman actually sits in the car and waits for her escort to come around and open the door for her. Some women still do that! On Park, Fifth, Central Park South, a woman does not hail a cab. The doorman hails the cab for her, and then escorts her to the car, holding onto her elbow as if she couldn't walk by herself, opens the door, closes the door.

It's the same routine when I let off someone. The doorman opens the door, holds on to her elbow, escorts her inside. When it's raining, the doorman comes with an umbrella, even when there's a canopy. And always, the doorman holds on to the woman's elbow. That would drive me crazy, someone holding on to my damn elbow every time I take a step.

PULLING IN

I love pulling in at night after work, all the cabs lined up waiting to go into the garage. Everyone gets out of the cab and starts rapping about how they did, what crazy passengers they had, where they had to go, what they ran over. Jake almost ran over a unicycle last night. I almost hit a kitten, and some other guy was talking about a trip through a cemetery in Queens.

Jake is the highest booker in the garage. They say that he has ESP and that's why he gets so many trips. But I did better than almost everybody these last two nights, since Jake took me aside and told me exactly where to go at what time so that I can make a lot of money too. He even took me out with him, told me to follow him in my cab and he showed me exactly the rounds he makes. "First, head for Fifth Avenue and pick up the shoppers coming home. Cruise Park and take couples to dinner. Are the shows letting out? Head for the theater district." He said I should always be thinking: "Where are the people? What are they doing now?" He's the kind of guy who just makes you smile and laugh and feel warm and good. Too bad he has a fianceé.

When we're in line waiting to get into the garage at night, Jake starts yelling, "What's going on, come on now, hurry up, hurry up, let's get a move on here!" in a Brooklyn accent. Then when it's his turn to move up, he's so busy rapping that he holds everybody up. Then the garage guys yell at him, "Come on now, let's get a move on here!"

When it's my turn, I pull into the garage. The mechanic opens the hood, checks the engine. I pull up further and he puts gas in the car. Then I go over to Sammy's booth where he sits above us all on an old cab seat. I give him my trip sheet. He adds it up and tells me what I owe him. I pull out my wad of money and hand it over. Then after I'm out of the garage, everybody's saying: "Who wants to go for coffee?" "Who's going to the subway?" "Who's going to the East Side?" "Who's going downtown?"

By 1:30 a.m. I am riding my bike home from work. I ride down Seventh Avenue and turn off near Greenwich Avenue and head east to 10th Street. The street is deserted and dark, except for a few street lights. Last night, I stopped on the corner of 10th Street and University Place, by Grace Trinity Church. There is a restored water fountain on that corner, so I stopped for a drink. Cold water. A boy on a bike also stopped for a drink. I had seen him ahead of me and he turned back when he saw me stop. We talked for a while. He wanted to race bikes down 10th Street, but I was too tired. He was riding with no hands, and I did do that. I couldn't do it as well as he could because I have a stupid girl's bike that doesn't have that bar. He demonstrated to me the "cool" way to do it

The "cool" way to do it is as if you don't have a care in the world, as if you aren't even thinking about riding down 10th Street with no hands, as if you know the bike is going exactly where you want it to go, without any effort on your part, just telepathy. He said the best thing would be to strap a radio on the handle bars and ride down the street clapping your hands. He demonstrated, clapping his hands and moving his body up and down as if he were really dancing to music, instead of riding a bike. When we got to my building, he asked to come up for coffee, but I told him my boyfriend was waiting for me. But now, I wish I had invited him up because it was fun talking to him.

HALLOWEEN

It's Halloween. All night long in the streets these little urchins with sooty faces would come up to the cab and say, "Penny! "Penny!" I gave a gang of four some apples I had just bought at the fruit stand. The kids looked disgusted and one little kid even gave it back to me and said he didn't want it. They just wanted money.

It's Sunday night. A drunk man wanted me to go to the Americana, pick up his bag, then take him to Penn Station. At the Americana, a group of men were hanging out looking for cabs, all of them were drunk. When my passenger returned with his baggage, I said, "Everybody's drunk tonight." He said, "What did you say, Dear?" "Everybody's drunk tonight!" "What did you say, Dear?" "Everybody's drunk tonight!" It surprised me because it's Sunday. Where I come from (Mount Healthy, Ohio), nobody even thinks to go to a bar and get drunk on Sunday. I think the bars might be closed on Sunday in Ohio.

My passenger thought I meant because Sunday is the Sabbath. "I know I'm a hypocrite. I've been a hypocrite all my life, but you, you know, Dear, one of these days, I'm going back to God, yes, I am, I'm going back to God, one of these days." I felt guilty for making this poor man feel guilty. He wasn't an obnoxious drunk, just drunk.

At Penn Station, a blind man climbed in. Took him to West 35th Street, where a deaf man flagged me down. He put a piece of paper onto the windshield with 42nd and Lex written on it. Then I got a guy on crutches, had to help him open the door.

The last fare of the night was a prostitute and two college boys I drove to a seedy hotel on the West Side. She sat in the front seat, the boys in back. She whispered to me, "This is a good way to get customers." She was young and pretty.

Cabs coming back to the garage were all soaped up and splattered with eggs. Tricks for no treats.

On my way home, riding my bike down Seventh Avenue, a newspaper flew right into the front wheel of my bike. I saw it coming. I saw the newspaper flying around the sidewalk. Then a gust of wind blew it out into the street. I thought it would lie there, but another gust suddenly came up and blew the newspaper smack into my front wheel. It got caught in the wheel. I keep on riding, leaning down to pull it out, but it stayed there, making a noise as the wheel turned, a newspaper noise. I could almost smell the newsprint. Finally, I got it out of the spokes and threw it on the ground, not the least bit guilty for littering. There's something about a newspaper flying on the street that is so Autumn in the City-ish.

TEMPTATION

This afternoon I had lunch at Luchow's. I went with Eugene, a guy I met at the Belmore (cabbie cafeteria on Park Avenue and 23rd, featuring free seltzer). I was sitting near him. It was about 12:30 or 1:00 a.m. He said, "I thought only cabdrivers came here." I said, "Well, I'm a cabdriver." He has called a few times and now this afternoon we finally got together. He's real nice, married, of course.

The reason Eugene is working as a cabdriver is because he was expecting to make $40,000 last year in his advertising agency, but only made $25,000 and got himself in debt. It turns out also he used to live in my neighborhood (East 10th Street). He grew up here. He's Ukrainian. He was brought up by his grandparents who hardly spoke English. He used to hang out at the Boys Club across the street from my building. His aunt owns the travel agency next door. He said at one time he needed confidence so he enrolled in one of those Dale Carnegie institutes. He needed knowledge so he enrolled in a speed reading course and bought an encyclopedia and was going to speed read all 26 volumes. He needed discipline, so he went to a hypnotist because he says discipline is just a matter of hypnotizing yourself.

Eugene said he enjoyed growing up on the Lower East Side. He thinks he had a lot more fun and had a lot more friends than his own kids have in the suburbs of Long Island.

He propositioned me. I mean a real proposition. He wants to sleep with me, but he wants to pay me for it. He suggested that I might like a few extra dollars so I could work less. We took a cab home from Luchow's—four blocks!

There's something wrong with this idea, but I can't put my finger on it. He says I might like to go to bed with him, and I might as well get some money for it. He likes the idea of paying for a woman. And now I'm thinking, gee, it might be nice to have a few men around like Eugene to take me out lunch, go to bed with for a few hours in the afternoon, earn a few bucks, give up cab driving. He says there are a lot of men who enjoy spending money on a woman. Eugene is not detestable. He's good looking.

When he realized I wasn't crazy about the idea of taking money from him, he said, "Let me buy you a stereo," since I told him, when we went to my apartment, that I didn't have a stereo. He also wants to buy me a radio. I told him I thought I was getting a radio for Christmas, from J.J., my now-and-then boyfriend. Eugene said: "What kind? I want to get you a good radio and a good stereo."

Since Eugene is married, he could never get to be too much of a pain in the neck. It would probably be just a luncheon thing. I keep thinking, "This is what the Bible means by Temptation." I am tempted to let him buy me a stereo. But how could I explain that to J.J.?

Knowing I have J.J. and knowing how hurt and upset he would be about the whole thing, really made me think twice. What would J.J. think if he knew his girlfriend was considering a career as a prostitute? The thing is, it doesn't seem so decadent me. And boy, did I ever eat at Luchow's! The bill came to $20! He invited me to a fancy lunch again tomorrow. I wanted to say, "Yes," but I said, "No." I'll see him at the Belmore.

Back in the cab, I daydreamed, looking back at all the opportunities that I have missed, the men who have tried to pick me up, in my cab, in bars. I wondered what would have happened if I had said, "Yes, but you have to make it worth my while," simply explained that I need money, and the man has money. It's as simple as that.

It's freezing in my apartment. The windows are closed and the heat is coming gently and slowly through the radiator. I am wearing long underwear, heavy socks and a heavy sweater. It is fucking cold in here.

CABBIE

There is a certain mystique to driving a cab at night. That's when the real cabdrivers work. Every Saturday, Sammy says, "Now, tonight, there's a million bucks out there." Out there, like growing on trees or something. In the day time, driving a cab is more like a milkman's job or a mailman's job. I'm making more money now than when I first started, instead of $25 a night, I make at least $30 (take home), and on Saturday night I can make $50, if I hustle.

There is a fraternal feeling among the people who work at jobs like this. A few days ago, I was stuck behind a truck. The truck was trying to park, but the guy in the street yelled to driver, "It's a taxi cab!" So the truck driver pulled over. "O.K., Cabbie, go!" Allowing me, the cabbie, to go through, while the other cars waited till he parked the truck. Today, I got stuck behind another truck. A policeman made the truck pull over. "Let the young lady make some money."

Say I'm cruising Park Avenue and I don't see a fare, but another cabbie does, and he already has a fare, he'll toot his horn for me so that I get the fare. I do the same thing, if I see a guy about to turn off the avenue, but there's a fare further down, and my cab is full, I toot and point out the fare. However, if there are two empty cabs and one fare, it is a real race. I am learning to cut off other empty cabs. It's a hustle, driving a cab.

There is the camaraderie of being working people, but there is also the feeling of being outsiders. For example, normally I wouldn't hesitate to go into The Plaza to take a piss, but driving a cab, I would not dare go into The Plaza. Normally, I wouldn't care if I had blue jeans on, but driving a cab, I feel self-conscious all of a sudden, even about going into some places on First Avenue. When you're driving a cab, you are really in a servant's class. I couldn't even walk in the front door of some apartment buildings on Park Avenue. Some? All of the apartment buildings. I would have to use the service entrance. I never thought of myself as a servant before. But that's exactly what I am, a servant to rich people. There are rich—and there are The Rich. My cousins in Ohio have no idea.

Saturday night I went to the West End, a bar-restaurant on Broadway and 113th Street where all the kids from Columbia hang out. I just went in to use the john. It's a cozy place and I always enjoy going there. But Saturday night just walking into the place made me depressed. All the people in there were Columbia students. They all had their notebooks with Columbia University stamped on them. They were ordering their evening meal. Many of these kids eat there every goddamn night! And I feel guilty when I buy a cup of coffee. Restaurant eating will probably always make me nervous.

So I was depressed realizing all these down-and-out looking kids were really rich. They eat at the West End, buy drinks, take taxis, pay Columbia's tuition, live on the West Side in nice apartments, buy books, don't work, go to classes and talk intellectual stuff over coffee. That's how they spend their time. Here I am driving a damn cab.

Despite being low on cash, I didn't work Sunday night. J.J. came over. The evening had a glow to it, beginning with hanging J.J.'s coat in the closet: soft lamps, incense burning, bowl of apples on the table, two coffee cups filled with fresh coffee, steam rising up. It was snowing outside. We rolled cigarettes, with fragrant tobacco I bought at the tobacco shop on 9th Street. We cracked walnuts and ate them intensely.

Then it felt good to be in bed, with fresh sheets and warm blankets. J.J. felt good. His skin is so smooth. He smells good. Not after shave, his body. He knows every bone, beginning with fingers, every fold, every crease of me above and below, in front, in back, between my toes, behind my knees. His legs are so long. We get tangled. I have to hold on to him. Who knows what would happen if I let go? I love when he says, with a grin: "O.K. now, turn over on your stomach. You start out with your arms around my neck all the time, every night, and every night you turn over on your stomach to sleep."

I sleep more easily when J.J. is here. I have to get a TV to keep him here more often. (It's football season.)

I told Eugene I had a boyfriend. Good thing. I might have been more tempted if I were all alone with no one to care what time I came home or if I came home or where I was when I wasn't home.

CABBIES DREAM TOO

Well, shortly after this trip to the john at the West End which brought me down, I had my own dinner break at the good old cabbie's diner on 86th Street and York Avenue. It brought me up a bit to see all the good old yellow cabs double parked up and down 86th Street, east of York. I walked in and sat at the counter. I bought a whole dinner, pork chops, beans, mashed potatoes, applesauce, milk and coffee. The guy next to me was reading *The Hot Seat* (newspaper of the Taxi Rank and File Coalition; see *Author's Notes*). I said, "Oh, you're a cabdriver, too." That started a conversation. He started giving me helpful tips. A guy sat down on the other side of me and joined in on the conversation. Soon all along the counter were cabdrivers, all giving me helpful advice and arguing among themselves about which ways are the best ways to make money driving a cab. All of the men chuckled a little about the idea of a "young girl" like me driving a cab.

They tried to explain how to fix the hot seat. When a passenger sits in the back seat, and the cabbie starts the meter, the light on the roof of the cab goes off. If an inspector sees a passenger in the back but the light is on, that means the cabbie is driving "off the meter," making money for himself that he doesn't have to share with the garage.

The guy to my right said he was writing *The Cabdriver's Opera*. He was giving me this whole spiel about how the cabdriver is the modern day cowboy when a guy came running in yelling, "The cops are ticketing the cabs!" Everybody jumped up, paid their checks, and ran out. My bill came to $2 including the tip, but what the hell. I took home one of the pork chops and had it for dinner again tonight. The opera writer yelled out to the owner: "What's the matter? The Knapp Commission getting to you?" The Knapp Commission is investigating bribery among policemen. It turns out that everyone in the entire police force has been taking bribes. (See *Author's Notes*.)

After work Dave and Richie from my garage took me out for a drink. They were darling, so careful about what kind of place to take me into. Dave is an ex-electronic engineer, Richie is an ex-math teacher. They both lost their jobs during the recession. At first they thought they had reached the lowest of the low points but then started to like driving a cab and were now making more money and having more fun and enjoying themselves. I believed them for a while. Dave is only 32 and looks 42. They both live in hotel rooms.

Richie got me a cab home. This driver also used to be an electronic engineer. Lost his job, but since he's an electronic engineer, he knows how to fix the hot seat and is making more money now. This guy has his own assigned car. He can take it home and park it outside his apartment and only has to bring the car into the garage once a week to give the owners the meter money. He had the whole cab fixed up like his own house: an ashtray attached to the meter, radio, plant, screwdriver stuck in the dashboard (for manipulating all the wires he has to pull). He told me he fixes the hot seat by pulling a certain wire, and fixes the light by pulling another wire (the hack inspectors check for the light on while the cab has a passenger), fixes the mileage with another wire. He had it all set up.

Tonight I took a cab home again. Richie walked me to the avenue—again. I don't mind somebody walking me to the avenue, but now Richie thinks I'm his goddamn girlfriend. I try to be as polite as possible. I told him I had a boyfriend; he still wants my phone number. I hope I don't have to come right out and say, "Fuck off."

Tonight's driver started telling me that the cabdriver is New York's ambassador, the first person a visitor meets in New York. The cabdriver listens to everyone's problems. In every movie about New York, this little yellow bug appears out of nowhere when you raise your arm, screeches to a halt, then turns around and drives off.

He told me he was coming over the Triborough Bridge one day in 1964 and saw a sign directing traffic to the World's Fair. Only through the haze he misread it and thought the sign said, "Drive a cab around the world to promote the World's Fair." He thought to himself, "What a fantastic idea!" He put his idea in motion, talking to everyone who got into his cab, making contacts. He met a rock singer who wrote him a theme song. The cabdriver proceeded to sing me his theme song, about driving a cab around the world to promote the World's Fair. He told me that he finally got his cab on a plane going to Europe. But his trip around the world in his cab to promote the World's Fair fell through in Paris. Two women had won the trip around the world in a cab as a prize, but had left because they thought he was a nut. Now he thinks his story is a multi-million dollar movie. He's looking for a screenwriter to write it and he's talking to everyone who gets in his cab about his idea. He also had a sign on top of his meter that said "Actor Available."

EVICTION

Usually when you are cold, you say to yourself, "Well, I'll be inside and nice and warm soon." But I am inside and I am freezing. Or you say "I'll close the windows and let the place warm up a bit." But the windows are closed, the stove is on. And I can't stop shiverrriiinnng!

I got an eviction notice Wednesday. I owe $220 (two months rent). At first, I didn't worry about it because I knew I would have $110 by the end of the week, when I went to work to pick up my check, and I could have the second $110 in three more weeks. But then February's rent is almost due. I didn't think I was worrying about it, but I couldn't sleep. I kept thinking, "What if they really do evict me?" The notice gave me only ten days and I could only pay $110 in ten days. I applied for a civil court trial to explain my situation (that I can't pay right away, but could pay later).

Well, my friend Tuohy, who lives in the apartment next door, thought I was being too indifferent about my situation. She lent me $120 (I had to pay an extra $10 for the repossession notice). It's a damn good thing because I finally realized how serious my situation was. They really were going to throw me out Monday!

I didn't ask Tuohy for the money. She suggested it, kept saying that I really should borrow money from her. She took the whole thing much more seriously than I did, and it's a good thing somebody took it seriously or I would be out on the sidewalk. Or in J.J.'s house. (I didn't mention it to J.J. He has his own problems.)

I can't get over how nice Tuohy was to lend me, and insist on lending me, $120. I went with my money order for $110 and her check for $110 to the landlord directly, again, on her advice. I was going to wait until Monday, and then mail the checks, but Monday would have been too late. Even today, they would not accept Tuohy's check. They wanted a money order, and I had to have it today because today is Friday and Saturday and Sunday the banks are closed, and Monday would be too late. So, I had to go back to Tuohy's bank, cash the check, and put it in a money order, go back to the landlord, pay everything.

Tuohy said not to worry about paying her back, to take my time. I think it's really nice of her because I can't think of too many people I would lend $120 to. She also lent me $10 to pay for the dispossession notice. And she gave me this money just like that.

LA FILLE MAL GARDÉE

One of my regular passengers (Wall Street-Park Avenue run) said I could have his two tickets to the American Ballet at City Center. Of course I invited Tuohy to go with me.

I took the cab out at 12 noon, came home and helped J.J. boost his car. When I left him this morning his car, parked on 10th Street, wouldn't start. It still wouldn't start so he had it towed to his garage and I drove him home (Queens) to watch the football game. We watched part of the game together and his mother made a good dinner for us. (His mother lives upstairs.) I went out to work finally at 3:00. I had to meet Tuohy on 10th Street at 6:00, but my last fare before picking her up was way up at 161st Street in the Bronx, so I had to come all the way down to the Lower East Side with no fare, because I was afraid of being late.

We drove to City Center, parked the cab at a taxi stand. We were supposed to find a lady in the lobby at 6:45 named Madelaine Cervantes and ask her for Bob's tickets. He had described Madelaine Cervantes as an old woman with wrinkles all over her face, gray hair and little, littler than me, and probably bundled up because it's cold outside. (It was so cold I had tears in my eyes.) We arrived at 6:45. Nobody was in the lobby, the show didn't start until 8:00. About a half hour later, people started coming in, checking their coats, talking about dance. "Did you see the last issue of *Dance* magazine?" "Oh yes, the article about Béjart and Nijinsky . . ." A woman who looked like a dancer said, "Madeleine..." I said, 'Oh are you Madelaine Cervantes?" No, she was not.

I asked every little old woman I saw if she was Miss Cervantes. By 7:45 the lobby was jammed and of course we still could not find Madeleine Cervantes. Everywhere people were trying to sell tickets for the night's performance, and we kept saying, "No, we're meeting someone here with free tickets for us." At the box office, the man couldn't remember any Cervantes picking up tickets. Or a Bob.

Well, 8:00 came and no Cervantes. The lobby was almost empty now. We didn't know what to do. We were just standing there. All of a sudden, out of the clear blue sky, an old man, who looked like a cabdriver himself, came straight up to us and said, "Here, do you want two tickets for tonight's performance?" We explained that we were supposed to meet somebody with free tickets for us, but they never showed up, and that we couldn't pay for them. He said: "I know, I know, these tickets are free. Take them and enjoy yourselves."

We couldn't believe it! We rushed up to the balcony and found our seats. After the lights went down, we moved up to the first balcony and could see fine.

La Fille Mal Gardée was just fantastic and magical and wonderful. Everybody in the audience liked it. It was funny. People laughed right out loud at the funny parts. I was so surprised. I didn't think it would be funny. In the intermission (the first one), Tuohy said, "I like ballet." I laughed because I knew she had just discovered ballet, just like I had, and was not expecting to find it so enjoyable.

It amazed me that something so traditional, so old, could be still so alive. All the dancers (I mean, the ballerinas) danced with satin blue and pink ribbons and wore pastel net ballerina costumes, except for the characters: the mother, the fool, the notary, the neighbors. There was the traditional *pas de deux* (a lot of them) and lots of solo dances, and suddenly a whirlwind of gypsy dancers. There was a real world on the stage, a complete environment. Maybe it was a magical world, but it was a believable magical world.

All the dancers took their bows in the positions of their characters. Even the bows got laughs. The fool (Alexander Filipov) made his entrances and exits for his bow just like the fool, and bowed just like the fool would bow. The young girl (Carla Fracci) made her exits and entrances and bows just like the naughty girl, and she looked like a naughty girl the whole time. The mother (Marcos Paredes) accepted her flowers with a curtsy, but for the third and fourth and fifth curtain calls, he bowed. Everybody got flowers. Everybody was screaming, really screaming: "Bravo!" "Bravo!" "Bravo!"

When the curtain finally was drawn for the last time, Carla Fracci came out in front of the curtain for another bow, and so did Marcos Paredes and Alexander Filipov.

The ballet didn't let out until 10:30. I drove Tuohy home and worked until 2:00 a.m. I was really afraid of going into the garage. The guy in front of me booked $54 and had been out since 5:00 (9 hours). I booked $34 and had been out since noon (14 hours).

Sammy was mad. He tried to bawl me out and I might get bawled out again when I go to work tonight, but I'm hoping he'll forget about it. The reason he couldn't bawl me out very well last night is because Jake was behind me and said: "Oh, she kept getting cut off. I know how it is. Every other cabdriver was cutting her off all night and picking up her fares. Isn't that right?" I nodded. Sammy growled, "I don't know what she was doing out there."

"She was getting cut off. I'm telling you. It happens to me all the time. It's a tough job, a tough job."

Jake walked me to the subway and I told him what had happened. He laughed and told me about the night he was out for 14 hours and booked four trips. He was fired and had to start working for another cab company.

These night hours are too much. I'm switching to days. Maybe I'll drop out of the working class for a while, go to graduate school. My shoes no longer look new, but well worn.

WINTER

I've started cooking oatmeal for breakfast, to give me energy since I'm driving days now. So I have a Quaker Oats box sitting on the shelf in the kitchen. Grade school teachers in Mount Healthy, Ohio, always had us bring in a Quaker Oats box to make things with. It was just assumed that everybody's mother cooked oatmeal for breakfast and everybody had a Quaker Oats box to bring in. Can't remember what we made.

I like the ritual of cooking oatmeal in the morning when it's cold and I'm still in my flannel nightgown and in the kitchen barefoot on the wood floor, striking the wood match to light the stove, stirring the oatmeal. It tastes just like childhood in Ohio. I put on my blue jeans and my work shirt, after scrubbing my face real clean and brushing my hair. I put on heavy wool socks because it's so cold outside and snowing. I listen to the weather report on the radio (I did get a radio for Christmas from J.J.). The weatherman reports that Central Park looks like a picture postcard, but it's a lot of work, everybody's out shoveling snow off the walks.

I like being awake and working at 7:00 a.m., wearing my work clothes, my work shoes, my pea coat, my cap and scarf, my wool socks and my wool vest. I like waiting in line at the Port Authority, reading *The Daily News*, drinking coffee and gabbing with the other cabbies. I like hearing people say "Good morning" all morning long, so that I really know it's morning. I like following the people. As Jake taught me, there is a pattern to people's movements in the city. At a certain time, go here, that's where people will be wanting cabs. At another time, go there. At one time, one place is busy as hell, an hour later, it's dead.

Central Park does look like a picture postcard, so white. The kids playing in the park in their navy uniforms look like a species of birds playing in the snow. Other little kids splash in the slush in the street, really enjoying using their boots for a purpose. A man crosses the street with a shovel over his back. Shopkeepers shovel up and down the avenue, women sweep after them. Everybody is bundled up, and me, nice and warm inside the cab, except for my wet and cold feet. I almost forget how cold and windy it is outside until I see a bunch of people clustered together at a bus stop shivering like hell, jumping up and down, holding their ears, scarves blowing, hair flying, coats flapping.

All the cabbies are trying, like I am, to keep their windows clean so they can see, picking up a handful of snow and washing windows with it, the ritual repeated at every red light. All the doormen on Park Avenue are out in their heavy uniforms and rubber boots shoveling snow. Everybody has on rubber boots today and I was noting all the different kinds. Little old ladies hold out their hands, and passing strangers help them onto the curb. Passengers all say, "How are the roads?"

I make three trips down to Wall Street, via the FDR Drive, race back up to Park, back down to Wall Street, up to Park, down to Wall.

I take my morning break at Horn & Hardart, the one on 45th Street and Lexington Avenue. Parking is reserved on that block for cabs. I pull up in front of another cab, another cabbie comes out of Horn & Hardart, makes preparations for driving away:

1. Takes off coat.
2. Washes windows.
3. Lays newspaper down on floor in back which is flooded from boots.
4. Turns on engine and lets car warm up.
5. Checks trip card, pencil, clock, radio.
6. Checks cigar box with money in it.
7. Puts on glasses.
8. Lights cigarette.

I like this Horn & Hardart because other cabbies come here, and I can always spot them. The coffee urn is coin-operated with fancy scallops on it. The handle is a knob on top of some kind of silver head. Three nickels in the slot, and coffee pours out of a silver mouth. (I'm in New York!) The cups and saucers are white with green lacy design around the saucer and the brim of the cup. Cushioned in the faux leather seat, I sit with my coffee looking out the huge windows at the snow, sunshine pouring in, watching cabbies get into the cabs and drive off, as other cabbies pull in.

I watch the women with children in the restaurant, the old businessmen reading *The Wall Street Journal* with their coffee, the young "in-training" businessmen taking a coffee break, the mailmen (the post office is nearby), and cabbies, recognized by their shabby clothes. I listen to the clatter of dishes.

After my break I cruise Broadway, north, away from midtown traffic, to get away from gas fumes. I have a dull headache from those fumes. At 113th Street an elderly man, with white hair blowing in the wind, hails me. "Oh, am I glad to see you!" he says in a beautiful accent, a theatrical accent that many people in New York have. I think he's a professor at Columbia. "We have to go over and pick up a lady—she just called me—and then take her to the doctor's." He must have dashed out of his apartment the moment she called. "Drive very carefully," he says. "Don't take any risks because the lady is sick." He eats a sandwich as I drive down Broadway.

We pick up the lady, a little old lady. The man is excited because evidently she called him in an emergency to escort her to the doctor's. "I am so glad I was home. . . Usually I . . . and then over to the university and . . . but I am so glad I was home to receive your call." He makes a big deal about her not wearing her rubbers. I pull over as close as I can to the curb because "the lady doesn't have her rubbers on." He goes around and gets in the cab from the street side because "I have my rubbers on."

On the way to the doctor's, he asks me to perhaps not stop in front of the building but up further, depending on where there is a clear space because the lady doesn't have her rubbers on and can't walk in the slush. We get to the address and the building has a doorman, who, of course, has shoveled off the sidewalk in front of the building so no one has to step in slush. The man carefully inspects the walk before signaling that I can stop there. "You can't walk in any slush, Dear. You don't have your rubbers on." The little old lady steps out of the cab and hits him with her cane, sputtering: "Will you shut up about the lady and her rubbers! I don't need rubbers! The lady doesn't need rubbers!"

The man tipped me very well and thanked me for driving so carefully.

DAY SHIFT

J.J. and I went to see Ike and Tina Turner at the Beacon Theater last night. What a show! It was packed and everybody was smoking grass. That woman is fantastic. When we got to the theater, there was a line all around the block. J.J. went right up to the front, in front of a little guy, we didn't want to get in front of a big guy. "Nancy, you just slide in beside me when I give you the word; we'll never get a seat waiting in this line." We got seats in the fifth row. I have never seen a woman dance like that before!

Got up at 6:30 a.m. I love pulling up the venetian blinds in the morning. (And I love closing the venetian blinds at night.) J.J. was here. It is so nice to get up together when it's cold out. Put on work clothes, made coffee. Made oatmeal for the two of us. Kissed J.J. goodbye and he went off to work. He's a compositor at a print shop on 8th Avenue. Sat down for another cup of coffee and a cigarette. That was a mistake since I was late for work.

It's about a half hour bike ride to the garage at 44th Street and Eleventh Avenue, uphill. It felt good to use my muscles. Got to the garage a minute before 8:00, locked my bike to the oil tank, went to the dispatcher's window. "Well, I don't know, Nancy. I don't have any cabs. Well, here's one but you have to be back by 2:00." Because it's some guy's steady car and he comes in at 2:00. I was being punished for being late, and also for not working this past weekend.

Warmed up the car, got settled, radio on the dashboard, coat off, pencil behind my ear, trip card and money in my cigar box on the seat beside me. Took off up Eleventh Avenue, got a fare right away, an old man and another old lady. I could tell he was a professor by his theatrical accent and also because he was carrying books and papers and wore glasses. He was quite interested in why I decided to be a cabdriver and we had a nice talk. He seemed to like young people in general. I concluded that he must be a favorite professor. The lady was charming too.

I spent the morning cruising the Upper West Side, which is slow compared to, say, Seventh Avenue. The problem driving a cab during the day is the traffic. Forget about driving down Seventh Avenue during the day. I read somewhere that one third of all the clothes manufactured in this country is manufactured in the garment district of New York City. From 42nd to 28th streets, cabs share Seventh Avenue with vans, buses, cars, pedestrians crowding the crosswalks, and young men pushing racks of clothes down the avenue all day. (See *Author's Note.*)

So I stayed uptown, and didn't get too many fares, but didn't get a headache from traffic fumes. I was driving on West End Avenue when a doorman hailed me. I stopped and he opened the cab door for another elderly woman, who carried herself like a queen. She wore a fur hat, a beautiful tweed coat, and nice leather boots. She also had an accent, a foreign accent, and a deep, rich voice. She wanted to go to New York Hospital. I think she was a doctor; she did not look like a nurse or a patient. She was large boned and tall, stately. When we got to the hospital, I got out of the cab and went around and opened the door for her. I felt like a tiny girl next to her. But she couldn't get the door open. This gave me a boost. I'm small, but I'm strong.

And so on for the rest of the day. Made two trips to LaGuardia and one trip to Kennedy and a $5 tip too. Every single passenger was nice. Everyone had a good conversation and everyone gave me a good tip.

Oh I've had a few bad customers, at night. A young man, in a sports jacket and nice shoes, who, when we arrived at Loews, opened the door for his date, then walked away without paying, with a grin on his face, thinking he had impressed his date by outsmarting the cabbie. What woman would be impressed by a man who stiffed a cabbie? How many times has a bartender thrown a drunk into the back seat, handing me an address scrawled on a napkin folded over some bucks (usually more than adequate). Once a drunk hits the cold air, he's out of it.

When I reach the destination, I try to stop under a street light because I have to get out of the cab and summon help from a passer-by (never a cop in sight) to pull the big lug out of my back seat. It's not safe to get out of the cab in a dark street that you don't know. Thankfully, no one has ever puked in my cab. But it happens. That's an advantage of driving in the day. The passengers are nicer.

My last passenger was a pretty grandmother and her pretty daughter, each cradling a tiny brand new baby in a tiny pink snowsuit. I picked them up at a doctor's office on Park Avenue and 32nd Street. They were going to East 71st Street. Normally I love riding up Park Avenue, through the tunnel and over the ramp and around the Pan Am building. But I was a nervous wreck driving with those two tiny babies. The cab seemed to be more jerky than normal. I was so aware that I had two newborns in my cab and God help me if anything went wrong. I almost ran into a bus, for instance, and another cab almost ran into me. Normally, that wouldn't phase me, but with two newborn babies in the back seat, I wanted a smooth and easy ride. We made it to the apartment on East 71st Street. The doorman fussed over them appropriately.

Went back to the garage, talked to some of the cabbies, cashed my check, and rode home on my bike, all down hill, from West 44th Street to West 10th Street, then through the West Village to the East Side. Now I'm having a Würzberger beer and a hand rolled cigarette. I had New York corn beef and cabbage for lunch at the Blarney Stone. So, I don't think I'll need dinner. I'm too tired to eat. There is a tiny, tiny bit of heat coming out of the radiator, just a slight warm draft by the bed.

STOPS ALONG THE WAY

I was coming up Broadway when a man hailed me at 78th Street. He said, "My wife will be out in a minute." I waited. His wife came out, carrying a small suitcase. I thought, "Oh no, I'll have to go to the airport." It was almost time for my morning break and I did not want to get stuck out in LaGuardia. Then I noticed that she was pregnant and walking slowly. I thought because of the snow, but no, she was very pregnant. I got the idea.

He helped her into the cab, and said, "O.K.! New York Hospital!" They were both smiling like mad, and I smiled too. I was nervous with the two tiny newborn twins, but this baby wasn't even born yet! The cab was so damn bumpy! The man kept saying to his wife, "Don't be nervous, Honey, don't be nervous." She kept assuring him that she was perfectly fine.

Well, wouldn't you know it. Turned into East 70th Street and got stuck behind a truck. My hands were so damn sweaty. Finally was able to back out into the avenue. My passengers were very nervous because they thought I would back into a car, which I didn't. I went around the block, turned into East 70th Street, from Second Avenue, and got stuck behind a bus! Finally got around the bus and we all breathed a big sigh of relief. Finally made it to New York Hospital. The man gave me a dollar tip. They were still smiling, smiling, smiling. A nurse came out and led the woman into the Emergency Room.

Didn't get to take my morning break until 11:00. Did not go to my regular Horn & Hardart, but to another one, on 45th Street and Sixth Avenue. I will compare them. In fact, I might make a study of all the different Horn & Hardarts in New York City. (See *Author's Notes*.) This Horn & Hardart also has revolving doors (two of them). I don't think I ever saw a revolving door in a coffee shop before I came to New York. This Horn & Hardart has very high ceilings, two stories high. I never saw a coffee shop with such high ceilings before. This one also has five high windows, as tall as the ceiling, morning sunlight streaming in. That's what I like about driving days, seeing so much sunlight all the time. There are bright orange, green, blue, and beige striped curtains on the windows.

The Horn & Hardart on Lex has only automat coffee. Here, you also get pies, cakes, bread and rolls, sandwiches from the automat, using coins that you put in the slot of the little boxes. Signs above the boxes indicate, PIES, CAKES, in special Horn & Hardart script. Overall, this restaurant is not as nice as the one on Lexington Avenue. The seats are not as nice. The plastic is cheaper and hideous colors (orange, green, blue) and torn in some places. It was 11:00 and ketchup bottles were on the tables, so it felt like an early lunch break, not a morning coffee break. The Lexington Horn & Hardart is cozier, because the ceiling is lower and the seats are a nice soft red, not McDonald's orange.

The customers are different too. Only two other women in the place, both old shopping bag ladies. The rest were old men and other cabdrivers, a few businessmen. The clientele at Lexington Avenue is more mixed, women and children, older business men and young businessmen, postmen and cabdrivers. It looked like all the customers in this place were cabbies, not bums, just a shade seedy. Still, it was comfortable and not at all a dive like the Horn & Hardart on 43rd Street or the one on 14th Street. That one is just revolting.

I think I'll make this Horn & Hardart, on 45th and Sixth, my alternate H & H, depending on which neighborhood I'm in at 10:00. I get a big kick out of putting the coins in the slots.

Sometimes I stop and get cigarettes at a candy store on Eighth Avenue. Inside there is a counter, but no stools. You can get an egg cream (a New York thing) and pretzels, and all kinds of cookies, big round cookies, plain cookies, chocolate cookies, chocolate covered graham crackers. You can get magazines and newspapers, and all kinds of cigarettes and tobacco, Zippo lighters, lighter fluid, cigarette holders, pipes, pipe cleaners, key chains, pens, Kleenex, combs, razor blades, cough drops, lifesavers, candy bars.

I went into this store on my way home from work yesterday. I was thirsty so I had a root beer and a pretzel and I bought *The Village Voice*. All around me people on their way home from work were stopping in before hitting the subway, buying egg creams and cokes and packs of cigarettes and the *Post*. Where but New York can you hear somebody say, "Gimme an egg cream" on their way home from work?

I discovered another Horn & Hardart when I was coming home from J.J.'s early in the morning and got off the subway at 23rd instead of 14th Street. In the subway is a Horn & Hardart. I went in to check it out. I was surprised because it was completely filled up with nice looking people. How did they find out about this Horn & Hardart underneath the ground? There is no entrance outside, on Park Avenue, only the entrance in the subway, before the pay booth and the turnstiles, so you don't have to pay 35 cents to enter the restaurant. No advertisements for this restaurant above the ground, no way of ever knowing about this Horn & Hardart unless you go down under the ground. So strange.

Another New York thing: Italian bakeries, with pastries and cookies in the windows and all different kinds of bread: round bread, oblong bread, flat bread, bread hanging, bread stacked, bread piled up in the windows.

And I will probably never stop smoking only because I love to go to the tobacco shop in my neighborhood and buy 25 cents worth of cigarette tobacco. The shop smells so good. Big barrels of tobacco. The man, wearing a cap like a taxi driver, lifts the lid of one of the barrels and measures out 25 cents (a half ounce) of cigarette tobacco on a scale, puts it in a bag and gives it to me. It smells so good.

And I live on a block that has a Russia Bath House, with a Ladies Day. And when school lets out, all the kids run up and down the block, jabbering away in Spanish. One pleasant thing about driving in the day is being home in the afternoon. Julia, the super's daughter, is practicing piano scales. The girl upstairs is practicing scales on the flute. Jeff, Tuohy's boyfriend, is practicing a blues scale next door. Throughout the building: C D E F G A B C D E F G A G F E D C B A G F E with a few flat notes thrown in.

My passengers say the reason I am so enthralled with New York is because it's still a novelty for me. They say, "Wait till you've been here ten years." But every once in a while I get a passenger who says, "Oh, New York is beautiful in the winter!"

MORE TEMPTATION

Yesterday I got up early and hopped on the train, one more trip to Brooklyn College. Took the Graduate Record.Exam. It wasn't too bad. Of course, the math part was horrible. But only one section was math. The English part was a breeze. I went over every question twice, and I was sure of every question, sure I was right.

Came home and paid my telephone bill. What a relief. Three more debts to pay off: Con Ed, this month's rent, and $120 to Tuohy, and I'm clear.

Today was the last time I ever work on Monday. It was dead. It was warmer today so I had the window open and I was breathing those fumes all day. Now I have a headache. That's the advantage of driving at night, a little more dangerous maybe, more rowdy passengers sometimes, but less fumes and more fares, more money. There is something about daylight, something about being awake at 7:00 a.m. But I am never working Mondays again. It's rotten. No business. One of the guys at the garage said, "Yeah, you have to have a sense of humor on Mondays."

Another girl showed up at the garage this week, Lin. So now there are two girls. Lin is gay. She sublets an apartment on St. Mark's Place. Her steady girlfriend, Gayle, still lives with her parents in New Jersey. We pulled in at the same time yesterday, so we walked to the subway together and rode the #6 downtown to Astor Place. I invited her over so she could finish the story she was telling me about her adventures with her Jane, a woman she picked up on Park Avenue who has a crush on her. She had spent the weekend with her.

She said she was in her fancy Park Avenue apartment and she got bored and wanted to so something, so she said, "I'm bored with you, let's do something." I said: "You said that? You said, 'I'm bored with you?'" Lin looked at me like I was an idiot. "Of course I said 'I'm bored with you.'" She dramatized, with her arm across her forehead, how she said: "I'm bored with you, I really am, Barbara, I'm bored. Let's do something."

So they went out to Barbara's house on Long Island. This chick had an apartment on Park Avenue and two houses on Long Island, and a chauffeured limousine. They went out to the house and fooled around, and then Lin said, "Well, I'm bored again." I asked her to say it exactly like she said it to Barbara. "Well (sigh), I'm bored . . . again."

Barbara said, "Listen, Lin, we'll do anything you want to do, anything, just tell me what you want to do and we'll do it." So Lin said she wanted to go to Southampton (she has another house in Southhampton), so the chauffeur drives them out there to a mansion. Nothing is on, no electricity, no heat. The caretakers come out to greet them. The caretakers' house is on the premises and everything is on in their house, but not in the big house. So the chauffeur goes out and gets them pizza to eat. They eat by candlelight. I am imagining a scene in a movie.

But Lin said, "You can't do this too long because you begin to get irresponsible."

"What do you mean?"

"Today is my first day at work in a month. That's bad. I really should work."

Lin said she really likes this woman a lot, and I can tell she really does like her. "But I've got to stop seeing her; it's too easy."

We started talking about people with money. It's so damn distracting to constantly see all these people with money. It's getting to Lin so much that she's trying to get another job, driving a school bus, that pays half as much, but is not so damn distracting.

The next day, I had an appointment with my ENT doctor. I have had a hearing loss since childhood measles. He propositioned me! He was probably half teasing and half serious. He said I could pay off his bill with a trade, two weekends. I owe $360 for an operation on my inner ear that was supposed to improve my hearing. The really strange thing is that Dr. M. is one person I would not mind spending two weekends with. I like him, and I have already thought to myself, how nice it would be to get to know him better. But I was thinking to get to know him like a daughter knows a father, or a niece knows an uncle. He's distinguished looking and he's important. He doesn't charge me for office visits. He knows I don't have the money.

To tell the truth, I would like to take him up on it, but I don't even know how to go about taking him up on it, especially since he says these things in a teasing way—and his nurse is always around. I'm sure he's teasing, but I'm also sure he's half serious. What a wonderful benefactor he would be. He's got money, and he's a lot nicer than Eugene.

His wife is a doctor too. She comes into his Upper East Side brownstone office in her fur coat, carrying packages from Bloomingdale's. She has blond hair that she wears up in a bun. She looks like one of the female doctors in a television series, always immaculate and fashionable, and she is beautiful. But I have never seen her smile. Dr. M. is always smiling and laughing.

But I can't imagine him in my Lower East Side apartment. He would not fit in. His bathroom is probably bigger than my whole apartment. I can't even imagine him walking down East 10th Street, with all the garbage cans and tenement buildings and fire escapes, and kids in the street.

I make him nervous. This is funny to me because I'm a plain Jane in blue jeans and hiking boots, with disheveled, mousy brown hair. I am skinny. I have that going for me. When I was in the hospital for the ear operation, he would make the rounds with all the medical students clustered around him in awe. The nurses treated me with meticulous care because I was Dr. M.'s patient, and he is particular. Yet I make him nervous.

I mentioned Dr. M.'s proposition to Lin, wondering if he had a chauffeur like her Jane, and how I might take him up on his proposition because I would really like a taste of the Ritz. Sometimes I think I don't want to be rich, but what the hell do I even know about it?

Lin said of course Dr. M. has a chauffeur. I said, "Hey, maybe I can get him to take me to lunch at The Plaza." Lin disapproved. I knew what she meant. "I'll get Dr. M. to take me to the Pierre." Lin said, "Very good."

Meanwhile, every night at 10:00 the boy downstairs comes home and turns his stereo on full blast. Mr. Blendowsky on the fifth floor yells, "Hey! What do you think this is, a concert hall?" The woman across the alley screams "Get off! Get off of me, you goddamn son of a bitch! Get off!" A beer bottle hits the brick wall, tinkles into the alley. Two cats screech horribly. The dog next door starts to bark. Mr. Blendowsky yells, "Shut that dog up!" An alarm goes off, an ambulance shrieks down the avenue. The stars prick the sky like pins in a voodoo doll.

BAD DAYS

Yesterday was the worst, absolutely the worst, day. First, a black cat crossed in front of my cab, the mangiest looking back cat I have ever seen. Then I got another parking ticket. I am pleading guilty with an explanation since I absolutely HAD to stop and take a piss. I just could not wait one second longer, not one more second, and just ran into the West End on 114th and came right back out immediately, and the man was filling out the ticket. I cried and followed him down the street crying.

"This means I worked the whole day for nothing! I can't pay this ticket! I don't make that kind of money! I'm just a cabbie. You know cabbies don't make no money. I had to take a piss. What was I suppose to do? I just had to take a piss!"

I'm certain I'll only have to pay $5, and not $25, if I go to night court and plead guilty with an explanation. Men always believe it IS an emergency when a woman has to go to the bathroom.

I have discovered that how to take a piss is the biggest concern of all cabbies, not just me. Luckily I have never pissed in the cab, but I have crouched behind the cab to piss in the street.

Later on in the day, I had parked the cab on East 10th Street and Second Avenue and went upstairs to my apartment to have some lunch, came back outside and had a flat tire. Called the garage and someone came down and fixed it. Was going to go back to the garage right way because it was 4:00 by this time and I was tired.

This job is a good job, except I can't make enough money, and I get very tired. The last hour is hell. The first hour is also hell. The hours in between can be enjoyable. Except for, as I said, not enough damn money.

I drove down 10th Street and as I was turning up First Avenue, the cab stalled. I put it in Park and started it up again. The cab jumped from Park to Reverse and I ran right into the guy behind me, another cabbie. He jumped out of the car yelling, "Everybody's driving a cab these days!" It turns out he had just had his car fixed and now I smashed it up again. He owned his own cab. The worst thing about this was that the accident was right on my own block where I live and he was making all this commotion and all my neighbors were crowding around and I felt horrible being so humiliated in front of my own neighbors.

I went back to the garage. While the other cabdriver and Sammy negotiated about fixing the car, I asked one of the guys if I could use the bathroom. He didn't know what to do. "The girl wants to use the bathroom!" All the guys hang out in the locker room. There is a long table where they play cards, lockers where they change clothes, sinks where they wash up after work, and bathrooms. I mean, johns and urinals.

All the guys had to clear out of the washroom so I could use the john. They had to interrupt card games, fling on shirts, grab towels, and everybody shuffled out into the front room while "the girl" used the john. When I came out, they all shuffled back in.

The garage is going to fix up this guy's cab, and everything's taken care of. God, what a day. After the flat tire I thought, "Well, at least I didn't have an accident today," and, what do you know.

On my way home I found a penny (good luck). Although the good luck has yet to appear. Of course, it might have appeared and I might not have known it was the good luck.

This morning I was met at the garage by a union guy, a fancy union guy in a suit and tie and tie clasp. The union guy wanted to inform me about the strike. He took me aside and explained the deal to me. He wanted to know if the boss had told me that I am only getting 42 percent, not 49 or 50 percent. I said, "Yes, but I don't want to go on strike." The union wants a strike, but I don't think the cabdrivers want a strike. I can't afford to go on strike. He said it would only be for a week, no longer than a week. If he already knows it will only last a week, why does there have to be a strike? Another cabdriver was there too and listening real close to what I said to the union man, if I would or would not go on strike. I felt like I was in a man's wheeling and dealing world, driving a cab, thinking about going on strike. What I want know is, why did the previous strike, last year, end up with a settlement of a 42 percent commission in the first place?

I told everybody in my cab about yesterday's adventures (ticket, flat tire, accident) and made fantastic tips all morning. I think I'll tell the bathroom story tomorrow, because people always ask me how the other cabbies take it, me, a girl, driving.

By 11:15, I had already put in a good three hours of work, when it started to rain. The windshield wipers didn't work very well, and I couldn't get the seat pulled up, so driving got very tedious. By noon I had a damn headache from those damn windshield wipers back and forth, back and forth, back and forth. When I pulled in that afternoon, sopping wet from the rain, but my feet dry as toast in my hiking shoes, one of the guys said, "This is the worst way to make a living, absolutely the worst." Everybody hated driving in that rain, not just "the girl."

Sammy said, "Don't say that to her; she might have had a good day."

"Naw, she didn't have a good day. Nobody had a good day today."

GROWING UP

The alarm went off at 5:25. I heard it and thought, "Oh, please, don't let it be 6:00 yet." It was only 5:25, I could sleep for another half hour. Went back to sleep till 6:15. Woke up and said to myself, "Well, now it's time to get up." I had every intention of getting up, but I didn't get up. It's not even that I said, "Oh, I'll sleep a few more minutes." I said, "Well, I'll get up now," and just did not get up. Don't know what happened. Finally woke up again at 10 to 7. I thought, "Well, maybe if I hurry I can still get to work on time." Got dressed, ate a bowl of corn flakes, rode my bike all the way up to West 44th Street. Got to work at 10 to 8. Left my bike unlocked in the yard. The yardman says: "Nobody'll steal it. You take the average guy here, the average guy here is too lazy to steal anything."

No car. Ten to 8 and no cars left in the garage. Another day of work missed. I was supposed to meet Tuohy for lunch, so I rode my bike over to Random House on 50th and Third. Tuohy is an editor and she's only 23. It was still not even 8:30 yet. I had to wait around till Tuohy came in to work at 9. We planned to meet for lunch. Went home, did grocery shopping, spent all my money just for fruit and vegetables and some cheese and milk.

On the way home, I saw Katherine running down the steps of the building, next door, with her German shepherd. When I first moved into this apartment last year, Katherine and Julia, the super's daughter, used to play all the time in the hall and make a lot of noise, like all kids. Katherine used to be a little girl, now she looks like a woman, tall and thin, with long blond hair, and so beautiful. She wears women's clothes now. This winter her coat is a brown fur maxi coat and she wears high brown leather boots with a heel, and one of those knit caps that are popular now. She looked so damn pretty with her coat and boots and cap and blond hair and her cheeks red from the cold. She looked like she should be walking out of a Park Avenue apartment.

She also made me feel like a slob. All the Polish girls in this neighborhood always look so damn neat and so pretty, and tall. I was thinking that Julia must feel funny, still being so young when her friend is getting older. Then I saw Julia coming out of the first floor apartment with her mother, and she is grown up too! She had on high boots with heels too! And she looked pretty too, not tall and willowy and blond like her friend. Julia is still chubby and short, but in grown up clothes she looked less chubby and more like a woman. Her face is losing its babyness. She is definitely catching up with her friend. Of course, neither of them ever play in the halls anymore.

All of a sudden these two little girls are grown up. You might think they were full grown women, but then the two friends started running and giggling down 10th Street like kids, leaving Julia's mother, a stout woman, walking slowly behind.

Filled out my application to graduate school, and now I'm waiting for $10 to fall in my hands, so I can send the damn application in.

"42 PERCENTER"

There may be a cab strike soon. The union is negotiating now. The strike is about the 42 percenters (the new drivers, like me, who only get 42 percent, not the regular 49 percent. This 42 percent thing was initiated by the last strike. I don't get it. The commission is lowered after a strike? There were cops all around the garage today. I was being called "a 42 percenter" instead of "the girl." I had planned to take tomorrow off. I am tired and sick too, another sore throat and cold and I feel like hell. I haven't been getting any sleep. Only four or five hours a night, and I really was counting on sleeping tomorrow, but I better go to work while I can. Besides, I have discovered that Sammy has been stealing from me. Fuck him! I'm going to start driving off the meter, a few fares, to get even.

Some of the 42 percenters on the evening shift didn't get cars. On a Friday night, the cars were just sitting there. Just what I need, a strike. Paid Con Ed bill today, finally, just in time to get the new bill for this month. Rent not paid yet and still owing Tuohy $120. Damn, I'll never get ahead of myself.

I'm afraid if I take a day off, Sammy might think I'm striking. I can't afford not to work. But when am I going do my laundry and wash my hair and clean the bathroom and dust and mop and clean my shoes and wash out my sweater and write to Aunt Dot if I have to work all the time? This is new for me, this worry about money and "job security" and paying the rent and getting evicted. A real worry, but still "interesting."

Sammy didn't say one word when I handed in my trip card all filled out in ink. Usually he fills it out and tells me how much I owe. Drivers are not suppose to fill it out. I didn't even ask, "How much do I owe ya?" I just handed him the money and didn't even wait for him to count it. Just left. He didn't say a word. Now he knows I've caught on. I was just waiting for him to say something so I could say, "Well, I think my arithmetic is better than yours."

PLANS

Today I got to work at 7:30, late. No more cars. Everybody's working. Nobody's on strike. I'm still a "42 percenter." They say it's Harry Van Arsdale's fault. And Mayor Lindsay. And Richard Nixon. Went to the garage around the corner. Got a car. This garage has hot seats so they always have cars. (Old timers don't like to drive hot seats.) And they are so damn polite. I couldn't believe it. They called me, "Miss Gerber," not "that girl." They thanked me when I gave them their money! And they smiled! They must really need drivers.

At my regular garage, it's "Where the hell were you this weekend?"

When Rocky gave me my trip card, he said, "Good luck, have a nice day." At my garage it's, "Make sure you're back by 4:30, Gerber."

At 4:00, when the shifts changed, and everybody was at the garage, coming or going, it looked like a regular hippie hang out. All these long-haired kids, and everybody with a paper-back book in his hands, hanging out in the garage, leaning against the wall reading. Not like the guys in my regular garage who are playing cards in the washroom or studying for the postal exam. One long-haired guy told me he reads while he drives, at stop lights. He said he reads 30 to 60 pages a day that way. In this garage, when someone is getting yelled at for not working weekends or for taking too many days off, the errant cabbie says, "I was studying" or "I had a paper due for school." Everybody has the same excuse: School!

I've also noticed a lot of long-haired mailmen around lately. Firemen too. I have to laugh when I see all these long-haired kids riding fire trucks and carrying mailbags.

Now I'm thinking of taking the postal exam. All of a sudden I realize what people mean by "plans for the future." Lin is also thinking about getting a new job. Sammy fired her. She went around the corner and now she's working for Rocky too.

But now she wants to be a police officer, an undercover agent, a narco. She said, "Well, I used to do a lot of heroin." Gayle, her steady girlfriend, laughed, "Yeah, Lin, you used to do a lot of heroin." Then hugged and kissed her because she can see straight through her.

We were hanging out at my apartment. I told them that the program director for "What's My Line" got into my cab Sunday. Now I'm suppose to meet her in her office and talk about being on the show. We started planning what I would wear. I have a long pale green skirt and jacket that I got at a thrift store. Better than my blue jeans. I'll wear my hair up. (See *Author's Notes*.)

My friend Steve came over. He's a classmate from my creative writing class at Brooklyn College, and the person who got me into being a cabbie in the first place. Hanging out after classes, Steve always had money in his pocket—because he was driving a cab, making tips every night. He persuaded me to try it. I took the mandatory class (was instructed to shower and to wear clean clothes). I passed the taxi exam (had to know how to get to Penn Station, Grand Central, JFK and LaGuardia airports, how to get across Central Park). I got my hack license.

But Steve doesn't want to be stuck driving a cab all his life either. He wants to be a lawyer and is taking a civil service exam to become a treasury agent, or something like that. He told me about a job opening for a lab technician at a high school in Brooklyn. I have all the necessary credits: 12 science credits (I have 16), 8 bio credits (I have 9). It's an easy job. Whatever you're supposed to do, you let a student do for you because the students love to do this kind of stuff (setting up equipment for laboratory experiments). You just sit in a room all day and read. The pay is $6,000 or $7,000 a year; the hours are 9 to 3.

Steve said I could definitely get this job but it just sounds so boring. One thing driving a cab is not, it is not boring. I'm not sure I want to sit with bottles of sulfuric acid in a high school classroom and I would still have to get up early to take the subway to Brooklyn.

So, what is my alternate plan? Be a school teacher, what else? A civil service job, that's what I need. Steady employment, etc. I'm thinking: "Gee, Nancy, why didn't you think of this before?" All the time, my family back in Ohio has been giving me this advice that I now discover for myself. All of a sudden I realize what people mean by "plans for the future." That phrase never meant one thing to me before.

We were all laughing so hard at ourselves. About how we have changed. Even Lin doesn't sit around and smoke pot all day like she used to.

I am going to apply for a mailman's job (if I don't go grad school). I think a mailman makes $3.65 an hour. All you do, you get your bag of mail and deliver it, and go home. And they have benefits, health care, retirement. Lin said: "That sounds too dangerous to me. A mailman could get mugged." We all laughed. She doesn't think being a narco—or driving a cab—is dangerous, but she thinks delivering mail is dangerous. Gayle said, "How many mailmen do you hear about who are killed?"

"Well, none."

"And you think being a mailman is dangerous?"

Lin said, "A cop carries a gun; he has protection, a mailman doesn't."

Neither does a cabdriver. Seven cabbies were killed last year, during holdups, for the 50 bucks (at most) in the cabbie's cigar box. (See *Author's Notes.*) Now, the fleets have plastic, bullet proof partitions between the front and back seats. Some cabs have locked boxes. My garage doesn't have locked boxes. We still use cigar boxes to hold our cash. Most of the cabs in my garage have the partition. (See *Author's Notes.*) No cab drivers have been murdered so far this year.

JUST WAIT

Steve came by last night because he wanted me to go with him to Bernadette Mayer's writing workshop at St. Mark's in the Bowery. I have been wanting to go to this workshop since I first heard about it, but the workshop has been in progress for several months, maybe it's too late. "Do you really want to go?" Steve asked. "Yes, I want to go." So, after Lin and Gayle left, we went up the block to St. Mark's.

We were late. About seven people and Bernadette were sitting around a table, in the middle of a discussion. Everybody knew everyone else. Steve and I walked in and sat down at the table. Steve had his book of poetry with him. We were sitting in the middle of an on-going discussion of an on-going workshop, not knowing anybody, but I, for one, and Steve, too, I think, felt perfectly relaxed in a few minutes, even though no one said a word to us. They didn't say, "Oh, hello, who are you?" They just continued with the discussion, which is probably why we felt relaxed. No one made a big deal about us suddenly appearing.

Bernadette gave an assignment: to write a poem invoking magic, a trance of some kind. Then she read a poem that did, in fact, put us all in a trance, about going down to the sea. (See *Author's Notes.*)

Steve and I are coming back next week. We couldn't stop talking about the workshop, how welcomed we felt, the poetry we were going to write. We were hungry so we went back to my apartment. I had a box of spaghetti and a jar of Ragu. My Aunt Dot keeps telling me I'll never find a husband because I can't cook. But I can cook spaghetti! I made the whole box. We ate from one big bowl, with chopsticks, sitting on the floor, crosslegged. He took the train back to Brooklyn at midnight.

So I didn't go to work today. Lin called at 7:30. I didn't hear my alarm set for 5. She was supposed to pick me up at 6:00 but called from Gayle's sister's apartment in Canarsie. I had to laugh because last night we both made such a big deal about working today. "You better be ready, Gerber," she warned me. I said, "I'm still in bed," and we both laughed.

My Aunt Dot sent me $25, birthday present. So I finally mailed off my grad school application. I thought about praying or meditating since I have nothing to do. This impulse usually comes on after I read the news. I feel an impulse to pray for peace for Ireland, for example, but then realize that God (if there is one) is not going to do anything about it. That's the secret of praying (or meditating, whatever you call it): don't ask for anything because that is hopeless. Just give thanks. If you want peace, you could meditate on the peacefulness of the church or the place where you are at the moment. Then, by concentrating on just that tiny space of peace in the church, the space grows, in your mind anyway.

J.J. came over to watch football. I see J.J. more often since Tuohy gave me her TV. She and her boyfriend, Jeff, are moving to Long Island. They're getting married! I finally paid back the $120. I don't think she even remembered that I owed her. Steve might come over again tonight. He doesn't like football.

Tuohy called to tell me that Shirley Chisholm is running for president! So I have been reading the papers all day and looking for the first sign of "Chisholm for President" groups because this woman does inspire me and I would like to work for her campaign. She's the first woman to run for the Democratic presidential nomination. (See *Author's Notes.*)

A woman in my cab the other day, an older woman, was asking me what my friends think about me driving a cab. "How do your friends take it?" I joked, "Oh they beat me up whenever they have run-ins with cabbies." What she meant was, "How do they take it since I am a woman." But I didn't realize this was what she meant until later. Or else I would have gotten into a woman's lib rap with her When she got out of the cab, she said: "You will see a woman president some day. Just wait. You will."

This thought thrilled and elated me! A woman president. She might as well have said, "You will be president some day." That's how the thought of a woman president affected me. A woman can be anything. I can be anything. Just wait.

AUTHOR'S NOTES

CABBIES DREAM TOO. From The Tamiment Library and Robert F. Wagner Labor Archives: "The Taxi Rank and File Coalition (TRFC), an organized group of disenchanted members of the New York City Taxi Drivers Union, Local 3036 was formed on April 15, 1971, in response to efforts by the leadership of the union and the taxi fleet owners to ratify a contract without a membership vote. For nearly seven years, the Coalition fought for a fair contract, better working conditions and a more democratic union. Members opposed what they saw as the autocracy of the founder of the union, Harry Van Arsdale, Jr." http://dlib.nyu.edu/findingaids/html/tamwag/wag_139/bioghist.html

See also: Richard Schlosberg (2019) The New York City Taxi Rank and File Coalition: 1971-1977, Labor History, DOI: 10.1080/0023656X.2019.166 https://www.tandfonline.com/doi/abs/10.1080/0023656X.2019.1666974

"What Frank Serpico Started: The Knapp Commission Report," by Tony Ortega, *The Village Voice*, April 18, 2011.

DAY SHIFT. For a history off the rise and fall of New York City's Garment District, see The Garment District Alliance at https://garmentdistrict.org or the Garment Industry History Project at https://www.gothamcenter.org.

STOPS ALONG THE WAY. For a brief history of Horn & Hardart in New York City, see "Before the Big Mac: Horn & Hardart," by Valerie Wingfield, Archives Unit, New York Public Library, December 8, 2010. https://www.nypl.org/blog/2010/12/08/horn-hardart-automats.

PLANS. I was a guest on "What' My Line." The panelists—Arlene Francis, Bennett Cerf, Dorothy Kilgallen—guessed my line pretty quickly. I won $50 and a Random House dictionary. My Aunt Dot and other relatives saw me on TV. So did my high school classmates. Even at my 50th high school reunion, classmates still talked about seeing Nancy Gerber on "What's My Line." My only claim to fame.

See "Attacks on Cabbies Laid to Militants; 7th Death Reported" by Edward C. Burks, *The New York Times*, August 27, 1970. https://www.nytimes.com/1970/08/27/archives/attacks-on-cabbies-laid-to-militants-7th-death-reported.html

The bullet proof partitions were mandated as a result of the taxi union action noted in "42 PERCENTER." So, drivers did get something.

JUST WAIT. See "Jan. 25, 1972: Shirley Chisholm Began Historic Campaign for President," Zinn Education Project. https://www.zinnedproject.org/news/tdih/shirley-chisholm-announces-campaign/ "Shirley Chisholm Runs for President,"

Women and The American Story. https://wams.nyhistory.org/growth-and-turmoil/ growing-tensions/shirley-chisholm-runs-for-president/ "Shirley Chisholm's Newly Unearthed 'Do Women Dare?;' Speech Is Just As Relevant Today" by Natalee Cruz and John Reed, *Rolling Stone*, February 3, 2022. https://www.rollingstone. com/politics/politics-features/shirley-chisholm-first-black-woman-congress-presidential-candidate-speech-1294152/

JUST WAIT. All these years I have remembered the poem Bernadette Mayer read in that workshop at St. Mark's in the Bowery. I have tried to find it, I have tried to remember it, have tried to write it—without success. One evening my husband Neal looked up from the *London Review of Books* to say, "I'm reading an article about Bernadette Mayer, and I think this is the poem you have been trying to remember."

The photo accompanying Janique Vigier's article ("At the Shrink," LRB, October 22, 2020) was Bernadette Mayer in the year she mesmerized us all by reading this poem that evening at St. Mark's in the Bowery. Here is part of it:

> *i'm going my way i'm getting along i'm going on i'm shoving off*
> *i'm trotting along i'm staggering along i'm moseying along i'm*
> *buzzing off i'm moving off i'm marching away i'm pulling out*
> *i'm leaving home i'm going from home i'm exiting i'm breaking away*
> *i'm o i'm setting forth i'm retiring i'm going down to the sea I'm*
> *removing i'm casing to be i'm disappearing i'm vanishing from sight*
> *i'm doing the vanishing act*

Bernadette Mayer died November 22, 2022. See: "Bernadette Mayer, Poet Who Celebrated the Ordinary, Dies at 77," by Alex Williams, The New York Times, December 4, 2022.

N. G. Haiduck is the recipient of the Jerome Lowell DeJur Award in Creative Writing from The City College of New York where she taught first-year writing students for many years. She has won the BRIO (Bronx Recognizes Its Own) Award from the Bronx Council on the Arts, and the Janice Farrell Poetry Prize from the National League of American Pen Women. She was a finalist for the Ed and Fay Phillips Prize in Poetry, Hannah Kahn Poetry Foundation. Publications include Aeolian Harp Anthology, BigCityLit, *Flying South, Hanging Loose, Main Street Rag, The Naugatuck Literary Review, Paterson Literary Review*, and *The Prairie Home Companion*. She is married to clarinetist Neal Haiduck. They now live in Burlington, Vermont.

www.ingramcontent.com/pod-product-compliance
Lightning Source LLC
Chambersburg PA
CBHW020240030726
47497CB00009B/3177